Welcome to
Hinch Farm

To Our Beautiful Boys,

Something for our family to cherish for years to come.
For us to read to you, for you to read to your children,
and for your children to read to theirs.

Ours may be just a story to some, but for us it represents the
most wonderful memories we are so blessed to share.

Everything we do, is for you.

For my wonderful family . . .
Alan, Sunny, Rory and Ruben (our cocker spaniel).
I couldn't love you more. xxxx
H.G.

PUFFIN BOOKS

UK | USA | Canada | Ireland | Australia | India | New Zealand | South Africa

Puffin Books is part of the Penguin Random House group of companies whose
addresses can be found at global.penguinrandomhouse.com.

www.penguin.co.uk   www.puffin.co.uk   www.ladybird.co.uk

Penguin
Random House
UK

First published 2023

001

Copyright © Mrs Hinch, 2023
Illustrated by Hannah George

The moral right of the author and illustrator has been asserted

Printed in Italy

The authorized representative in the EEA is Penguin Random House Ireland,
Morrison Chambers, 32 Nassau Street, Dublin D02 YH68

A CIP catalogue record for this book is available from the British Library

ISBN: 978–0–241–56960–3

All correspondence to:
Puffin Books, Penguin Random House Children's
One Embassy Gardens, 8 Viaduct Gardens, London SW11 7BW

Mrs Hinch

Welcome to
Hinch Farm

Illustrated by
Hannah George

PUFFIN

In a lovely red-bricked house, there lived a family who loved to play, go on adventures and spend time with their friends. For Mum, Dad, Ronnie, Lennie and Henry, it was SO much more than just a house – it was their **HOME.**

It was where they
cuddled on the sofa
to watch movies . . .

where they ate all of
their favourite dinners
(sometimes accidentally
dropping the best bits on
the floor for Henry) . . .

and where they
always returned after
fun family trips.

Kitchen

Bathroom

Lounge

Shoes

But **EVERYTHING** was
about to change.

Mum and Dad told them they were
moving to a new house. It sounded
very exciting, but as the boxes piled up,
the brothers became a little nervous.

BEEP! BEEP! BEEP!

came the sounds of a big truck reversing.

Henry, Ronnie and Lennie rushed to the window
to see where all the noise was coming from.

They watched in confusion as Mum and Dad began
to load the truck with boxes. Today was moving day.

"DON'T WORRY, BOYS! Everything is going to our new house! We'll unpack as soon as we get there and it'll feel *just* like home."

TOYS

The thought of their things in a new house felt strange to them.

Suddenly, Henry whimpered and rushed out to
the back garden. His brothers chased after him and
quickly realized what he was worried about.

Their beautiful Wendy house. Would that be coming too?
Henry looked at Mum with big, sad eyes, but she shook
her head. "Sorry, darlings – that has to stay, I'm afraid."

Soon, the house was *completely* empty.

Henry sniffed at the bare room.
The boys had never seen their home
like that, and it was a little scary.

"Let's take a little walk through the house
one last time and say thank you for all the
fun times it's given us," Mum said.

So they thanked each room
for the special memories
they had made there.

Henry hoped there
would be time for
one final play
in the Wendy house,

but suddenly it was time to go.

Later that afternoon, they arrived at their new house.
"Welcome to Hinch Farm, boys!" said Dad. "Our **NEW** home!"

The brothers glanced at each other
nervously. It wasn't the same as their
old home. It looked different . . .
Sounded different . . .
And Henry even thought
it smelled different . . .

Hinch Farm

As the day went on, the boys tried *really* hard to settle.
But when Ronnie wanted to play with his diggers, they weren't
in any of his boxes.

Lennie couldn't find his book about rabbits.

And Henry sniffed high and low for his
chicken sticks, but they were *nowhere* to be seen.

The next morning, sunlight poured in through the window.

The brothers smiled at each other and stretched –
this was **PERFECT** weather to play in their Wendy house!
But then they remembered where they were. This was the new house,
and they had left their beloved Wendy house behind!

Henry's head sunk as the boys thought about their old home.

They missed it **SO** much.

Ronnie hugged Lennie and Henry nuzzled into
them both, but it didn't help. Nothing felt right.

Suddenly, Henry jumped up. He had an **IDEA!**

They should visit their old home and have one last play in the Wendy house. Ronnie and Lennie began dancing in excitement.

Henry wagged his tail and then started running in circles round his brothers. It was great to see Ronnie and Lennie smile again!

Ronnie found some paper and pencils,
and the boys started to make a plan.

Henry watched as his little brothers drew all the things they remembered passing in the car.

Before they knew it, they had a map that would lead them back to their old house!

Ronnie snuck into the kitchen and packed one apple, two chocolate bars and three lollipops for their adventure – plus some ham for Henry!

They each thought of the fun they would have in the Wendy house. Henry was looking forward to eating the chicken stick that he'd buried under a bush.

The boys set off through the front door. They tried to open the heavy door *reeeeeeally* quietly, but . . .

"WHERE ARE YOU GOING?"

Mum and Dad heard the door and ran down the stairs!

They looked down at the boys' coats and the map
in Henry's mouth . . . and understood.

Mum wrapped the boys up in a big hug. "You miss the old house, don't you? It's OK to feel that way," she said.

"Change can be unsettling, but what will never change is how much we all love each other. So maybe we can help each other love this new house, too?"

Dad put on some music and they danced around while they unpacked.

Ronnie found his diggers . . .

Lennie found his book about rabbits . . .

and Henry found the stash of chicken sticks that Mum had been hiding.

The house was starting to feel like home.

"Great work, my boys!" said Dad. "Now I've
got a surprise to show you. Come with me . . ."

Dad led the boys out into the garden, and their eyes grew as big as saucers. In front of them stood an **AMAZING** treehouse!

It was just as amazing as their Wendy house,
except it had legs and was high up in the sky!

"We haven't forgotten you, Henry," said Dad, as he handed him a new rope toy to play with.

Henry stretched out on the patio happily and watched over his brothers playing. Seeing them laugh together gave him a warm, happy feeling. And as the sun started to set, he had an idea . . .

Henry pushed everyone into the house and on to the sofa.
"Henry wants something, don't you, son?" said Dad.

"I think I know what Handsomes wants!" said Mum with a smile.

Mum and Dad got some tasty snacks ready
and put on their favourite film.

Cuddling all together on the sofa like old times, they all came to the same realization – what makes a house feel like home is family.

Change can be scary, but with their family always
by their side, the Hinch brothers can do anything.

Hinch Farm